D1278696

Wake Up, Bertha Bear!

by Chad Mason
Illustrated by Chad Wallace

Down East Books
Camden, Maine

To every child who has known the hurt of being passed over when teams are chosen. Don't give up.

—C.M.

In loving memory of my friend Daphne Pouletsos and all the other victims of the attack on the World Trade Center on September 11, 2001.

—C.W.

Text copyright 2005 by Chad Mason
Illustrations copyright 2005 by Chad Wallace

Design by Lindy Gifford

ISBN 0-89272-655-5

Library of Congress Control Number: 2005928857

5   4   3   2   1

Down East Books
Camden, Maine
A division of Down East Enterprise, publishers of Down East magazine

To place a book order or to request a catalog, call 800-685-7962 or visit www.downeastbooks.com

Printed in China

On a wooded island in the middle of a lake, Bradley
Bear and his mother, Bertha Bear, slept in their
warm, cozy den. It was April, and spring
had come to the north woods.

Bertha Bear snored very loudly. The noise woke up Bradley, and he felt hungry. Bradley had been born in January and had never been outside the den. He had grown fat on his mother's milk, but now he wanted solid food. "I'll go outside and look for something to eat," thought Bradley.

Outside the den, the sun was bright. The ground was wet. The air was warm. Bradley could not hear his mother snoring any more. He could only hear birds singing.

"It's a fine day," Bradley thought. "I'll find some yummy bugs to eat. Then I will come back to the den."

But Bradley could not find any yummy bugs on the island. So he went across the lake on the melting ice, hopping from chunk to chunk. He hopscotched a long way and finally reached the shore of the mainland.

Bradley walked into the woods and discovered a hollow log on the ground. It was soft and black. And it was loaded with yummy bugs. Bradley sat down and ate until his tummy was full. When he had finished, he felt very sleepy.

Bradley thought, "I'll take a little nap before I go back to the island." So he climbed into a fir tree, where the soft needles would keep him warm and cozy. Then he fell asleep. He slept and slept . . .

. . . for two whole days.

When Bradley woke up, he could not remember where he was. He was too afraid to climb down out of the fir tree, so he began to cry. He cried and cried.

Fritz Fox heard Bradley Bear and came to have a look. He saw Bradley in the fir tree. "Little bear, what's wrong?" he shouted. But Bradley just kept crying.

Stanley Skunk also heard Bradley and came to have a look. "Hello, Fritz," said Stanley. "Why is that little bear crying?"

"I think he's lost," said Fritz.

"Where is his mother?" Stanley asked.

"Perhaps she is still asleep in her den," said the fox.

"Perhaps someone should find her and wake her up," said the skunk.

Fritz thought for a moment. "I have a plan," he said.

"Can I help?" asked Stanley.

"No, thanks," said Fritz. "All you know how to do is stink. But I know just who we need." Then Fritz Fox went to get help. Stanley Skunk's feelings were hurt, but he followed far behind and watched.

Fritz Fox found Walter Woodcock, who had just returned from his winter home in the South.

"What do you want?" Walter grumped.

"I need your help," said Fritz. "I know that you can hear things under the ground using your feet."

"Yes," said Walter, "that's how I find worms to eat."

"Well," said Fritz, "do you think you could hear a bear snoring in her den?"

"Sure I could," huffed Walter Woodcock.

Fritz Fox told Walter Woodcock about Bradley Bear and the plan to find his mother.

"But how will you wake her up?" Walter asked.

"Don't worry," said Fritz. "I know just who we need. Come with me."
So Fritz Fox and Walter Woodcock went to get more help.

Stanley Skunk followed far behind and watched.

Fritz Fox and Walter Woodcock found Loretta Loon. She was sitting on a rock, sunning herself and feeling pretty.

"What do you want?" Loretta sighed.

"We need your help," said Fritz. "We know that no one can croon like a loon, and you are the loudest loon around."

"Yes," said Loretta, "that's how I tell other loons where I am."

"Well," said Fritz, "do you think you could wake a sleeping bear?"

"Sure I could," answered Loretta Loon.

Fritz Fox told Loretta Loon about Bradley Bear and the plan to find his mother.

"How will you know where to look?" Loretta asked.

"Don't worry," said Fritz. "I know just who we need. Come with me." So Fritz Fox, Walter Woodcock, and Loretta Loon went to get more help.

Stanley Skunk followed far behind and watched.

Fritz Fox, Walter Woodcock, and Loretta Loon soon found Rodney Raccoon. He was washing his hands and getting ready to eat his dinner.

"What do you want?" asked Rodney.

"We need your help," said Fritz. "We know that raccoons are fine sniffers, and you are the finest one in these woods."

"Yes," said Rodney, "that's how I find my food."

"Well," said Fritz, "do you think you could sniff out a bear cub's trail?"

"Sure I could," said Rodney Raccoon.

Fritz Fox told Rodney Raccoon about Bradley Bear and the plan to find his mother.

"Let's go!" said Rodney.

So Fritz Fox, Walter Woodcock, Loretta Loon, and Rodney Raccoon went back to Bradley Bear's tree.

Stanley Skunk followed far behind and watched.

Rodney Raccoon sniffed out Bradley Bear's trail, and the others followed. Soon they came to the lake. All the ice had melted.

"The trail ends here," said Rodney. Fritz Fox thought for a moment. He knew that baby bears did not come out of lakes. Then he looked across the water and saw the island.

"The island!" said Fritz. "That's where Bertha Bear always spends the winter. That little bear must be Bertha's new cub. I bet he came across the ice."

"Well," grumped Walter Woodcock, "now what?"

"Don't worry," said Fritz Fox. "I know just who we need. I'll be right back."

In a few minutes, Fritz Fox found Molly Moose, who was munching on soft grass.

"What do you want?" Molly mumbled.

"I need your help," said Fritz. "I know that you are a very fine swimmer."

"Yes," said Molly, "that's how I get away from flies when they bother me."

"Well," said Fritz, "do you think you could swim all the way to the island?"

"Sure I could," said Molly Moose.

Fritz Fox told Molly Moose about Bradley Bear and the plan to find his mother. "Let's go!" said Molly.

Soon Fritz Fox and Molly Moose joined the other animals by the shore. "Climb aboard!" Molly said, and she bowed low to the ground. Fritz Fox, Walter Woodcock, and Rodney Raccoon climbed over Molly Moose's big head and across her neck onto her back. The moose then splashed into the water and swam toward the island. Loretta Loon swam along beside her friends.

Stanley Skunk sat on the shore and watched. He felt very sad and lonely and left out.

Molly Moose and Loretta Loon quickly reached the island and climbed onto shore. Fritz Fox, Walter Woodcock, and Rodney Raccoon jumped off Molly's back.

Walter Woodcock began hopping around in the woods and listening with his feet.

"Over here!" he called. He was standing on a small, rocky mound. "She's right under my feet!" he said.

The others quickly found the door of Bertha Bear's den.

"Okay, Loretta," said Fritz Fox, "give her all you've got!"
Loretta Loon stepped up to the den and cleared her
throat.

"AAHH–LAH–DEE–LAH–DEE–LAAAAHH!"
Loretta cried loudly. But there was no answer. Bertha
Bear was still sound asleep.

"AAHH–LAH–DEE–LAH–DEE–LAAAAHH!"
Loretta cried again. But once more there was no answer.

"She's still snoring," said Walter Woodcock.

All the animals sat down to think. They didn't know what to do.

Suddenly, Molly Moose had an idea. "I've got it!" she shouted. "I know just who we need! I'll be right back."

She ran to the lake, jumped in, and swam toward the shore of the mainland.

Stanley Skunk sat at the water's edge. He still felt very sad and lonely and left out. When he saw Molly coming, he stood up.

"We need you, Stanley!" Molly called out.

"What?" asked Stanley. "Are you sure you really need me? All I know how to do is stink."

"That's just why we need you," said Molly as she reached the shore. "We need smelling salts. Climb aboard!"

Stanley Skunk jumped for joy. Then he climbed onto Molly Moose's back, and off they went to the island.

Once on land, Molly Moose brought Stanley Skunk to Bertha Bear's den.

"Of course!" shouted Fritz Fox. "Smelling salts!"

"You can do it, Stanley!" they said.

Stanley lifted his tail and shot his strongest smell into the den.

Everything was quiet. All the animals waited and then…

A loud roar came from the den. Bertha Bear was awake! She came out grumpy and rubbing her eyes with her big paws.

Then she heard something on the breeze, far away across the lake. It was the sound of a little bear crying.

"Bradley!" Bertha exclaimed. She ran down to the lake, jumped in, and swam toward the sound of the cub's crying. Molly Moose followed, with Fritz Fox, Walter Woodcock, Rodney Raccoon, and Stanley Skunk riding on her back. As before, Loretta Loon swam along beside.

When Bertha reached the shore, she ran to the big fir tree that Bradley Bear had climbed. The cub was so glad to see his mother that he jumped out of the tree, right into Bertha Bear's arms.

The other animals cheered. Then Fritz Fox said, "I know just who we need. "Who's that?" the other animals asked.

Fritz Fox put his hand on Stanley Skunk's shoulder.
"We all need each other!"